REAL LIFE HEROES

SURVIVING CANCER

REAL LIFE HEROES

SURVIVING CANCER

Jane Bingham

ARCTURUS

This edition first published in 2010 by Arcturus Publishing
Distributed by Black Rabbit Books
P.O. Box 3263
Mankato
Minnesota MN 56002

Printed in China

Series concept: Alex Woolf
Editors: Alex Woolf and Sean Connolly
Picture research: Alex Woolf
Designer: Ian Winton

Library of Congress Cataloging-in-Publication Data

Bingham, Jane.
  Surviving cancer / Jane Bingham.
    p. cm. -- (Real life heroes)
  Includes bibliographical references and index.
  ISBN 978-1-84837-694-6 (library binding : alk. paper)
  1. Cancer in children--Juvenile literature. I. Title.
  RC281.C4B555 2010
  618.92'994--dc22
                                    2010014145

Picture Credits
Corbis: cover (Steve Nagy/Design Pics), 7 (Photo Quest Ltd/Science Photo Library), 8–9 (LWA-Stephen Welstead), 13 (Karen Kasmauski), 19 (Darren Kemper), 21 (Richard T Nowitz), 22–3 (Jim Craigmyle), 27 (Hola Images), 32 (Dan McCoy – Rainbow/Science Faction), 34–5 (Image Source), 36 (Ted Spiegel), 41 (Inspirestock).
Getty Images: 15 (rubberball), 25 (Tom Raymond), 31 (Paul Spinelli/MLB Photos), 38 (Rob Meinychuk).
Science Photo Library: 11 (Steve Gschmeissner), 12 (Sam Ogden), 17 (CNRI), 18 (GCa), 24 (Dr P Marazzi), 28–9 (CC Studio), 33 (Samuel Ashfield), 40 (Du Cane Medical Imaging Ltd), 42 (Simon Fraser/Royal Victoria Infirmary, Newcastle).
Shutterstock: 6 (pixinity), 10 (Brad Wynnyk), 16 (Shawn Pecor), 37 (Elena Elisseeva).

Cover picture: A young cancer patient.

SL001047US   Supplier 03 Date 0510

Contents

Introduction

Most young people don't think of cancer as something that could ever happen to them. But some unlucky teenagers do get cancer. In the United States, one in every 330 children will develop cancer by the time they are 20. Every day in the UK, up to six young adults between the ages of 13 and 24 will find out that they have some form of cancer.Fortunately teenage cancers can usually be treated, and many young patients recover completely. In this book you can read the inspiring stories of young people who have battled with cancer and survived.

What is cancer?

Cancer is a disease that affects the body's cells. Every part of your body (including your blood, your skin, and your organs) is made up of tiny cells that can only be seen under a microscope. When these cells are healthy, they make your body function normally. But if the cells become cancerous, people soon begin to feel very ill. If the cancerous cells are not destroyed, they can spread fast and overcome the healthy cells in the body. However, there are several ways to kill cancer cells (see page 8).

Cancer types

Experts have identified more than 200 types of cancer, which can affect many parts of the body. Some of the most common forms of the disease are cancer of the breast, lung, and colon, but these types of cancer are usually found in older people.

▲ Roughly one in 500 young people will develop some form of cancer before they are 25. However, the survival rates are getting better all the time. It is estimated that around 75 percent of young people with cancer will recover and go on to live a healthy life.

In many forms of cancer, the cancerous cells form a tumor (or lump). This is often the

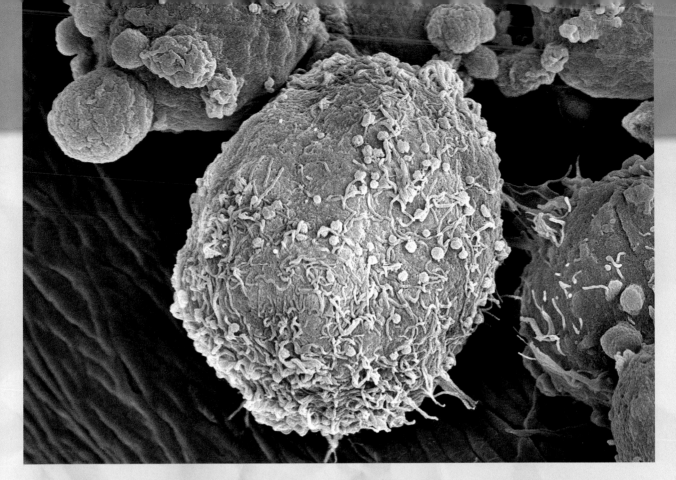

▲ A highly magnified cell from a patient with a lymphoma. Like all forms of cancer, lymphoma causes the body to develop abnormal cells, which replace the normal, healthy cells. Lymphoma usually starts with a lump in the neck, armpit, or groin. It generally affects children and teenagers rather than adults.

first sign that something is wrong. But not all tumors are cancerous. Doctors investigate any suspicious lumps to discover whether they are cancerous or benign (harmless).

Teenage cancers

The most common cancer among children and teenagers is leukemia, a disease that affects the blood (see panel on page 11). Teenagers can also suffer from osteosarcoma, a cancer that attacks the bones of growing girls and boys (see page 18). Some teenagers develop lymphoma, a disease of the lymph system inside the body (see panel on page 23 to learn about lymphoma and the lymph system). Another, less common form of cancer in teenagers is cancer of the brain (see page 26). This book describes the experiences of young people who have suffered from all these types of cancer.

Why do people get cancer?

A few types of cancer have been linked to people's way of life. So, heavy smokers run a high risk of developing lung cancer, and too much sunbathing can result in skin cancer. However, these kinds of cancer only affect adults because they take a long time to develop. Most teenage cancers have no obvious causes.

Treating cancer

The thought of cancer can be frightening, but the facts are often less scary than people think. Thanks to modern medicine, many forms of cancer can be treated—especially the kinds that teenagers develop. Cancer specialists (known as oncologists) use three main methods to destroy cancer cells: surgery, chemotherapy, and radiotherapy.

Surgery involves operating on a patient to remove a cancerous tumor and the body tissues surrounding it. Chemotherapy uses a combination of medical drugs to destroy the cancer cells, and radiotherapy involves the use of high-energy X-rays directed at the part of the body affected by cancer. These methods of treatment can have very good results, and they are all described in this book.

Helping recovery

It is very important to get the right medical treatment, but people with cancer can also do a great deal to help themselves. Following a healthy diet and getting lots of rest helps patients to make a good recovery.

Most people who are diagnosed with cancer find it is very helpful to understand exactly what is happening to them. This can be done by talking to nurses and doctors and other trained staff and by looking at reliable websites (see panel). When you understand the medical processes that you are going through, it can help you to feel a lot less afraid. It can also make you feel much more positive about your treatment and its outcome.

Sharing experiences

Learning how others have coped can be very helpful. If you are just starting out on a course of treatment, it can be comforting to hear from someone who has completed the course and is now well on the way to recovery. Of course everybody's experience is different, but there are still many things to share.

Help and information

There are many excellent websites providing information on cancer and its treatment. Some of these sites are specially designed for teenagers and include a forum where young people with cancer can share their feelings and experiences. There are also many local groups, offering help for people with cancer as well as giving support to their friends and family. Turn to page 45 for a list of helpful websites.

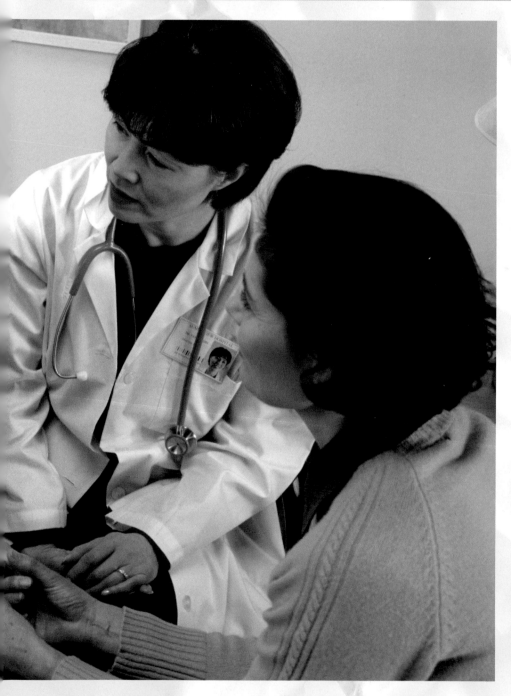

The stories in this book describe what happened to ten young people who faced cancer—either coping with the disease themselves or helping a member of their family—and who all came out the other side. The stories are true, but people's names and some aspects of their identity have been changed.

◀ When a young person is diagnosed with a cancer, the news can come as a horrible shock. But talking things over calmly with an expert is very helpful. Doctors can help patients and their families to understand more about their disease and the kinds of treatment they will receive.

Jemma's Story
Overcoming Leukemia

It all began in the summer vacation, when Jemma started feeling tired all the time. She had always had plenty of energy, so she was confident she would soon feel better. But when she started saying no to parties, her friends were surprised. Maybe there was something really wrong with her.

Worrying signs

As the weeks went by, Jemma's exhaustion got worse. She had a summer cold that she couldn't shake off, followed by a throat and ear infection. Then she started getting lots of bruises. She told herself that she was just being clumsy, yet secretly she was very worried.

Time for action

On the morning before the family vacation, Jemma woke up feeling terrible. She forced herself to get up and start packing, but she soon collapsed back into bed. By lunchtime she was running a fever and vomiting. Her mom decided it was time to take action.

A phone call to the family doctor was followed by an emergency appointment. It was not the first time Jemma had seen him that summer, but this time she listed all her symptoms, and he looked very serious. "I want to send you to the hospital for some blood tests today. And I think you'd better put off your vacation."

Change of plan

Jemma and her mom would never forget the next few hours: the drive to the hospital, the tests, the waiting, and the

◄ For some cancer patients, the first sign that there is something wrong is a feeling of exhaustion. Boys and girls who have always had lots of energy may start to feel tired all the time. In many cases, the feeling of tiredness creeps up gradually, as everyday living becomes increasingly hard.

Leukemia

Healthy blood is made up of three main elements: red cells, white cells, and platelets. Each of these elements plays an essential part in keeping you well. Red cells carry oxygen to your muscles so that they can work. White cells fight infections. Platelets help your blood to clot and form scabs. All three types of cell are constantly dying and being renewed by new cells. The new cells are made in the bone marrow inside your bones.

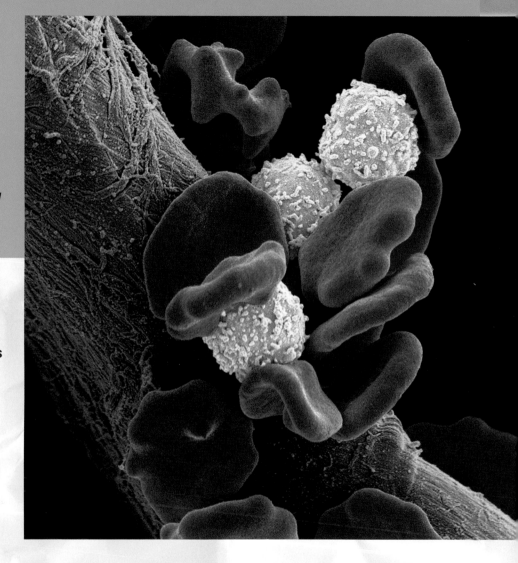

▶ **This photograph shows a sample of blood from a patient with leukemia. It has been magnified more than 2,000 times, and the cells have been brightly colored to make them easier to identify. The sample shows red blood cells and cancerous white cells.**

meeting with the doctor who gave them the results. "We suspect that you have leukemia, and we want to admit you admitted to the hospital."

The next morning Jemma woke up in a hospital bed. Instead of setting off for a summer vacation, she was preparing to fight for her life.

When people have leukemia, their bone marrow produces abnormal white blood cells, which multiply very fast and crowd out the healthy cells in their blood. Without enough red cells in their blood, people get tired and achy. A lack of healthy white cells makes them vulnerable to infections, and the reduced number of platelets results in nosebleeds and lots of bruises.

Tests and treatment

Once she was admitted, Jemma faced a series of tests. The biggest of these was a lumbar puncture, which involved extracting a sample of her bone marrow to see how advanced the leukemia was. At the same time her doctors started her on an intensive course of chemotherapy to destroy the abnormal cells in her blood.

Within a few days Jemma had grown used to her new routine. She was taking up to 30 pills a day for her chemo treatment and was sleeping a lot to recover her strength. When she first arrived on the ward, she had been given a single room. This was because her white blood cell count had dropped so low that she was in danger of picking up infections. It felt strange being on her own, but the hospital staff were friendly and kind, and her mom and dad came to visit every day.

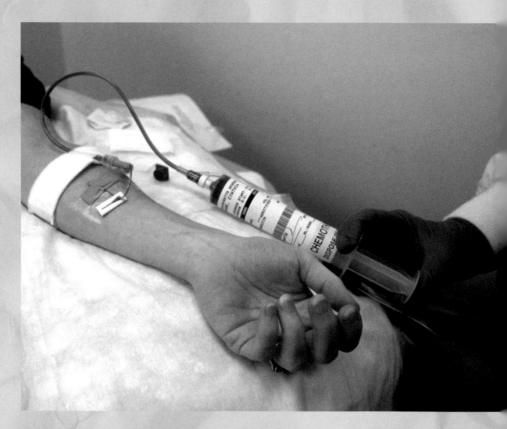

▲ Chemotherapy drugs can be delivered in a range of different ways, according to the patient's needs. Here, a nurse uses a syringe to inject the drugs into a patient's arm. The drugs enter the patient's veins and immediately get to work, fighting cancer cells.

Coping with chemo

As well as swallowing pills night and day, Jemma also had some sessions of intrathecal chemotherapy, in which a combination of cancer-fighting drugs was injected into her spine. Her doctors explained that this procedure was essential to kill any cancer cells that might have spread to her brain and spinal cord. Jemma found that she could cope with these sessions if she visualized the good drugs spreading through her body and zapping out any bad cancer cells.

Side effects

After a few days of chemotherapy, Jemma began to notice some unpleasant side effects. She developed ulcers in her mouth and was very weak. She often felt sick and had to force herself to eat. But the thing that upset her most was losing her hair, about two weeks into

Chemotherapy for leukemia

Chemotherapy uses a combination of medical drugs to destroy the cancer cells. It can be delivered in three main ways. Patients may take tablets or capsules. They may have injections into the area around the spinal cord (intrathecal injection). Or the drugs may be delivered through a tube that is attached to part of their body, such as their chest.

her treatment. "I always knew that I would lose my hair, but that didn't stop it being a shock. My beautiful long, dark hair was falling out in clumps."

Jemma's treatment did not go entirely smoothly. There were a couple of scares when she developed serious infections and had to be given extra antibiotics to fight them off. But after about a month of intensive chemotherapy, she began to feel stronger. Her doctors reported that the treatment had destroyed 90 percent of the leukemia cells and she had reached the partial remission stage.

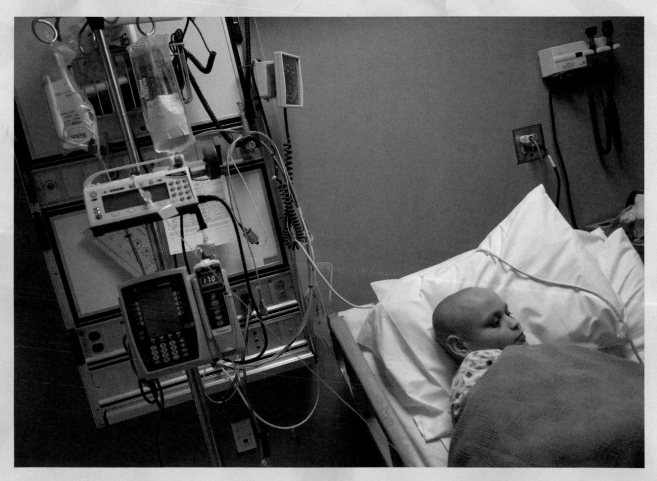

▲ When patients need large doses of chemotherapy, they sometimes have a tube attached to their chest. This allows the drugs to be delivered slowly over an extended period of time.

Getting stronger

Once she was no longer at such high risk from infection, Jemma was moved into a general ward. She was fortunate to be in a large hospital that specialized in teenage and childhood cancers, so there were plenty of people of her age. It was a great relief to be able to talk to other teens who had been through a similar experience, and over the next few months she made some very good friends. "I could share everything with my friends on the ward. There were some tears, and plenty of hugs and jokes."

Home and hospital

Over the next few months, Jemma continued her chemotherapy and gradually grew stronger. When she first became ill, she had lost lots of weight, but now she began to fill out again. She also began to make some visits home. The first time she went home she was so excited she could hardly sleep the night before. But the visit ended badly as she developed a very high fever and had to return to hospital for intensive treatment.

Despite these setbacks, Jemma continued to make good progress. As she grew stronger, she spent longer at home, taking charge of her own medication. Eleven months after she was first diagnosed with leukemia, her doctors declared that she was in remission. Their tests had shown that she was completely free of cancer. As Jemma remembers, "It was the best news I had ever heard in my life."

Surviving cancer

Jemma was fortunate. Three years after she began her hospital treatment, she has stayed in remission. Today she is healthy and active again, but she is not likely to forget her experience with cancer. "Surviving cancer has made me feel grateful to be alive. It's stopped me from taking anything for granted and made me concentrate on the really important things. Having cancer when I did made me into the person I am now—someone who is determined to live every day to the full."

Three-stage treatment

Treatment for cancer usually happens in three stages. The first, known as induction, is a period of very intensive treatment to stop the cancer from spreading. The second stage, known as consolidation, aims to destroy all the cancer cells in the body. When this is achieved, the patient is in remission. The third stage, known as maintenance, is not always necessary. It is much less intensive and is designed to keep the patient free from cancer.

▶ *(Opposite)* Cancer patients sometimes need to spend several months in the hospital. In the first weeks of intensive treatment, they may have to stay in bed most of the time. Later, they can be more active.

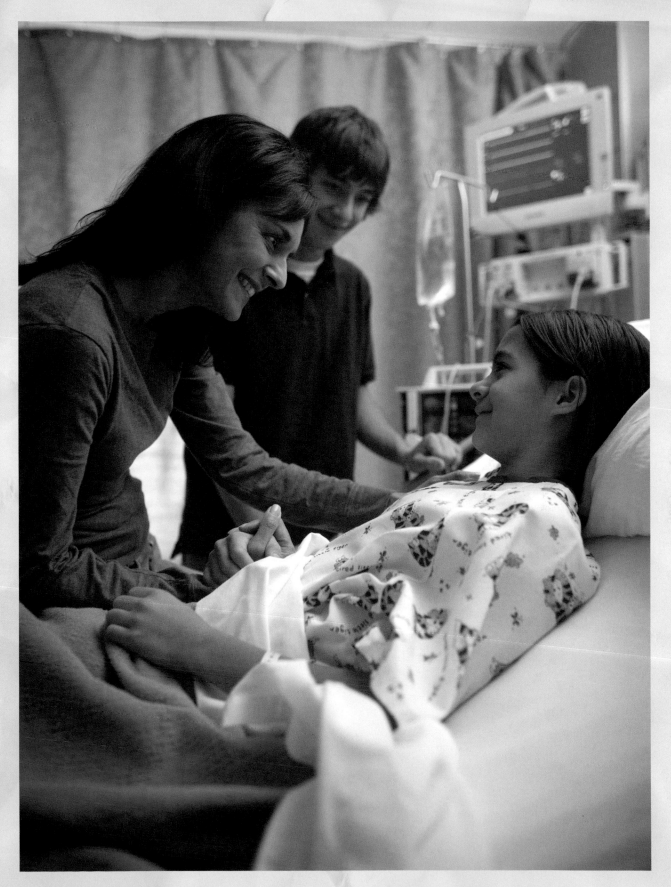

Ben's Story
Surviving Osteosarcoma

Ben had always excelled at sports, and by the age of 12 he was winning medals for sprinting. But when he sprained his knee, soon after his 13th birthday, it didn't get better. This was the first sign that Ben was suffering from osteosarcoma, a form of cancer that attacks the bones.

Strange symptoms

Nobody thought at first that Ben's painful knee was anything serious. He had suffered bad injuries before and had always bounced straight back. But as the weeks went by the pain grew worse and worse until it started keeping him awake at night. He began to walk with a limp and he noticed an unusual lump just beneath his kneecap. When he showed the lump to his doctor, she thought that it was probably harmless. But she sent him to see a specialist—just in case.

Scans and tests

At the hospital, Ben was given an X-ray, followed by a series of scans. By the time his leg had been scanned by a CT machine and an MRI scanner it was clear that he had some kind of problem, but it was still a shock to hear the diagnosis. The specialist said he suspected

◀ Osteosarcoma (cancer of the bone) can affect healthy young people. It is more common in boys than girls, and it often occurs in the teenage years. The cancer usually starts with a tumor on a leg or arm bone. If the tumor is not removed, the cancer can spread rapidly through the body.

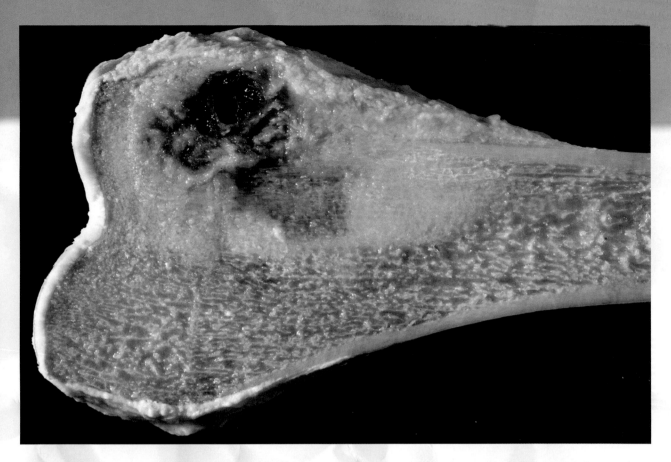

▲ A cross section of a shin bone with a cancerous tumor. Surgeons treating osteosarcoma need to cut away all the diseased parts of the bone. Sometimes a bone can be reconstructed. In other cases, the affected part of the patient's limb has to be amputated.

that Ben had a cancerous tumor. But first he needed to perform a biopsy—a small operation to remove some cells from the tumor, so they could be examined under a microscope. The biopsy would show whether the tumor was benign (harmless) or malignant (life-threatening).

All sorts of scans

Oncologists (specialists in cancer) use several different kinds of scanning equipment to give them the information they need. X-ray machines produce a photograph of the bones in the body and are very useful for identifying tumors. CT machines create a three-dimensional image to help build up a more precise picture of a tumor. MRI scanners produce a very accurate image of a bone and the muscles surrounding it. They can show whether the tumor has spread into the surrounding tissues.

Bad news

On the day of his appointment with the specialist, both Ben's parents came with him to the hospital. When the doctor explained the results of the biopsy, the news was bad. Ben had osteosarcoma, a cancer that causes tumors to form on the bone. The cancer had spread to his muscles and he needed immediate treatment to save his leg. For the boy who had always dreamed of being a top athlete, the future looked grim.

Osteosarcoma

Osteosarcoma is the most common type of bone cancer. It usually develops from the cells involved with bone growth and it commonly affects teenagers when they are experiencing a growth spurt. Tumors occur most often in the longer bones of the body, such as above or below the knee or in the upper arm near the shoulder, and they are more common in boys than girls. There is currently no effective way to prevent osteosarcoma, but with proper treatment most patients recover and learn to use their limbs again.

Treatment and surgery

Ben was admitted to the hospital, where he started a course of chemotherapy to kill the cancer cells and to shrink the size of his tumor. Meanwhile, his doctors took scans of the rest of his body to make sure that the cancer had not spread. Then Ben was prepared for surgery to remove the tumor on his upper shin.

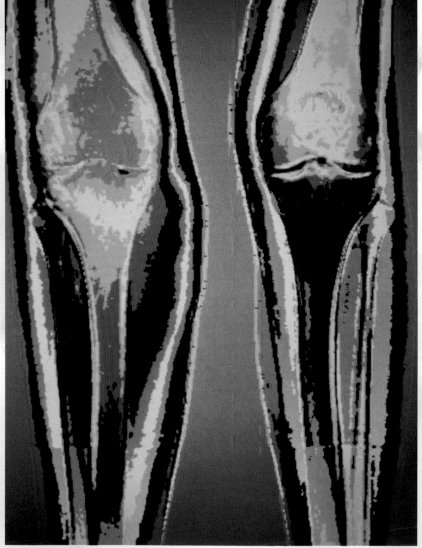

When surgeons operate to remove a tumor on an arm or leg, they always try to save the patient's limb. Limb salvage surgery involves removing the bone and muscle affected by cancer and then filling the gap with a bone graft or with a special metal rod known as a prosthesis (or prosthetic device). After examining the scans, the surgeon decided it should be possible to save

◀ A CT scan of a patient with osteosarcoma in the upper shin bone (on the left-hand side of this image). The cancerous tumor is colored green. You can also see the swelling of the tissues around the tumor.

▲ Learning to walk after major surgery is difficult and exhausting. It can take months of exercise and therapy to build up the muscles in the legs. And the challenge is even more daunting for people who want to return to playing sports.

Ben's leg. Once he had removed all the cancerous bone and muscle, he inserted a metal prosthesis, connecting Ben's kneecap to his lower shin.

After the operation

Ben's operation went well, but this was just the start of his long, slow progress toward recovery. He had to continue with his chemotherapy to make sure all the cancer cells were destroyed, and he also had to learn how to use his "new" leg. After major surgery, it is very important to keep the muscles working. So, within a few days of his operation, Ben was attached to a continuous passive motion (CPM) machine, which continuously bent and straightened his knee. As soon as he was strong enough, he started on an intensive course of physiotherapy to teach himself how to walk again.

Learning to walk

For the first six months following his surgery Ben needed a walker or crutches to get around, but then he was on his own. Progress was painfully slow, as the boy who was once the fastest runner in the school struggled to cross the room without help. But the same determination that had made him a champion sprinter helped him succeed in the most difficult challenge of his life—and within a year he was walking well.

Problems and setbacks

Ben's recovery was not completely straightforward. Very soon after his operation he developed an infection around his wound, and for a while it seemed as though his body would reject the metal prosthesis. Also, because the rod was inserted when Ben was only 13, he faces the prospect of a second operation to fit a replacement when he has finally finished growing. But Ben is determined to overcome all obstacles. "I've got so far," he says. "Nothing is going to stop me now."

Sporting hero

Ben certainly has traveled far and fast. Not only has he learned to walk again, but he has also returned to sprinting. Less than two years after his operation, he was competing in races for disabled athletes. He has had to work very hard to build up the remaining muscles in his lower leg, and he keeps up a tough training routine, exercising in a gym and running every day. He even has plans to go skiing next year.

Encouraging others

Three years on from his first diagnosis, Ben still visits the hospital where he was treated, to encourage young patients in their recovery. He is a popular visitor on the ward, where he loves to share a joke with everyone. For those who are coping with the challenge of becoming mobile again, Ben's achievements provide a great source of inspiration.

Prosthetic devices

A prosthesis or prosthetic device is an artificial replacement for a leg or an arm or a part of a limb. Modern prosthetic devices to replace part of a bone are usually made from a lightweight titanium rod, which is connected to the patient's own bones. Sometimes people with osteosarcoma need to have most of their limb amputated. They can be fitted with an artificial arm or leg that has been designed to perform the same functions as a natural limb. Some prosthetic arms and hands are covered with soft plastic and can look very realistic.

Ben also visits the hospital for regular check-ups to make sure that his cancer has not spread. Young people who have had osteosarcoma have only a 60 to 80 percent chance of remaining cancer free, so he knows that he may have to face more treatment some day. However, he is very optimistic about the future. "Once you've proved that you can beat cancer, you know that you can tackle anything life throws at you."

▶ *(Opposite)* **Modern prosthetics are very lightweight and are designed to act just like natural limbs. It is even possible to play basketball while wearing a prosthetic leg and foot.**

Ellie's Story
Living with Lymphoma

Life was going well for Ellie. She had recently moved to a different school and had made some great new friends. So when she noticed some worrying symptoms, she told herself she just didn't have time to be sick. Eventually, however, she had to face the fact that she could be seriously ill.

Feeling unwell

Over the course of two or three months Ellie began to feel increasingly unwell. She felt tired most of the time and got out of breath when she climbed the stairs. Her skin was itchy and she sometimes woke up at night covered in sweat. She knew that something wasn't right, but she tried to persuade herself that all these things would pass. Then, one day, she felt a painful lump on the side of her neck that she just couldn't ignore. It was time to visit her doctor.

Worrying results

Ellie's doctor listened carefully to all her symptoms and took a sample of her blood to be tested. Ellie imagined it would be some time before she heard any results, but her doctor was in touch within a couple of days. She said that the tests had shown up some worrying results. Could Ellie please go to the hospital the following day for an appointment with a specialist?

After that, things happened very fast. At the hospital the doctor performed a biopsy on

The lymph system and lymphoma

The lymph system works as part of the body's natural defense against infection and disease. It is a complex system that includes the bone marrow, the spleen (a small organ on the left-hand side of the body), and a set of lymph nodes throughout the body. Lymph nodes are also known as glands and are most obvious in the neck, armpits, and groin (at the top of the leg). The nodes are all connected by a network of tiny tubes known as lymph vessels. When someone develops lymphoma, cancer cells grow and multiply in the lymph nodes and are sometimes visible as lumps. Because all the lymph nodes are connected by vessels, lymphoma can spread rapidly through the body.

the lump in Ellie's neck and sent off some tissue for tests. Ellie was also given a series of scans to check whether she had any more lumps in her body.

"You need treatment straight away"

After two days of tests, the doctor made his diagnosis. He explained to Ellie that she was suffering from lymphoma, a kind of cancer that attacked the body's lymph system (see panel). The scans had revealed that as well as the lump in her neck, she had tumors in her chest, which were making her breathless. She needed treatment straight away.

◀ There are two main types of lymphoma (cancer of the lymph system): Hodgkin's lymphoma and Non-Hodgkin's lymphoma. In cases of Hodgkin's lymphoma, the cancer tumors are usually easy to destroy using chemotherapy and radiotherapy. Patients with this type of cancer have a 90 percent recovery rate, so long as the tumours are found early enough. The tumors in Non-Hodgkin's lymphoma are harder to treat, but can still be destroyed.

Starting the treatment

The specialist told Ellie that she would need a long course of chemotherapy, which would last for around six months. Every two weeks she would come for a session at the hospital, but for the rest of the time she would be at home. She could even keep going to school, so long as she felt up to it. She was fortunate that the lymphoma had not spread below her chest, so she had a very good chance of recovery.

Ups and downs

After three months of chemotherapy, Ellie's tumors had reduced in size and her symptoms had begun to disappear. Three months later the doctors' scans showed that all the cancer cells had disappeared. Ellie knew that she should be delighted, but something bothered her. She had a nagging feeling that the lymphoma had not completely gone, and two months later she was proved right when she found a new lump on her neck. Ellie remembered that day as a very low point. "I wasn't sure then that I would ever recover."

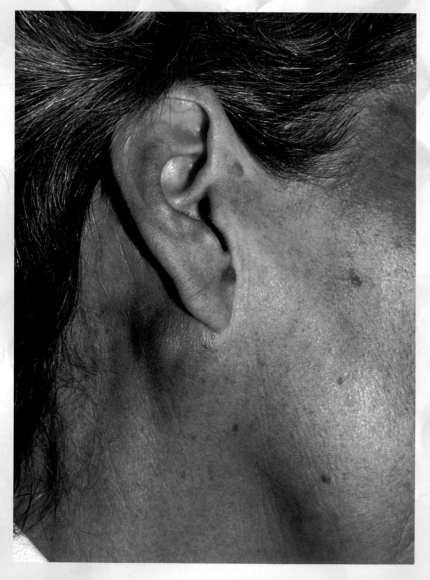

So, instead of returning to school as she had hoped, Ellie started on a second course of chemotherapy, this time followed by a month of radiotherapy to make sure that the cancer did not return. By the time her treatment was finished she was exhausted, but she was determined to see it through. "I just wanted to be completely sure that there were no more cancer cells left inside me."

◄ **This cancer patient has a lymphoma tumor in the lymph gland behind her ear. Lymphoma tumors can be destroyed by an intensive course of chemotherapy. It is also very important to make sure that the cancer has not spread to other lymph glands in the body.**

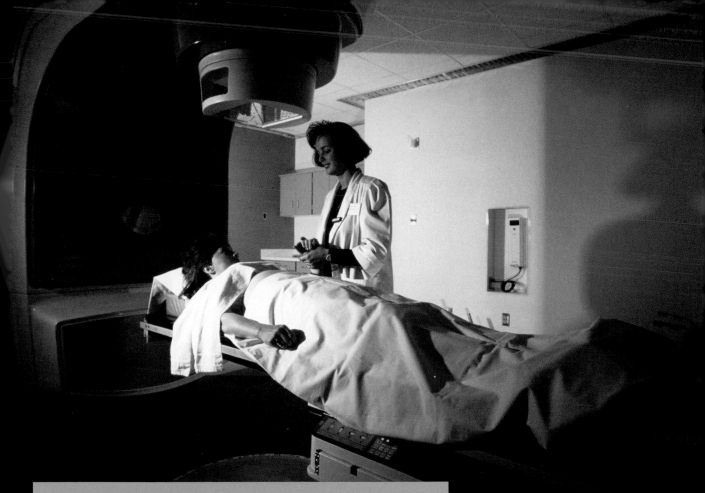

Radiotherapy

Radiotherapy is the use of high-energy X-rays to destroy cancer cells. The treatment can be delivered from outside or inside the patient's body. External radiotherapy is used for cancers that are close to the surface of the body. It is delivered by a special machine that directs X-rays to the area affected by cancer. Internal radiotherapy is used for treating cancers deep inside the body. In some cases some solid radioactive material is inserted close to the tumor for a limited period of time. In other cases a patient is given a radioactive liquid, either as a drink or as an injection into a vein.

▲ A patient is put at ease by her doctor before receiving external radiotherapy. Many cancer patients need a course of radiotherapy after their chemotherapy is completed. This is to make completely sure that no traces of cancer are left in their body.

All clear

After the radiotherapy, Ellie was given the all-clear once again, and this time her scans have stayed clear. During the past two years, she has returned to the hospital for regular checkups, which have all shown that she is in remission. She has also joined a special partnering scheme in which people who have had lymphoma get together with someone who is currently being treated for the disease. "I was lucky to beat lymphoma," she says, "and I want to help others to do the same."

Amit's Story
Beating Brain Cancer

Amit is a lively and popular teenager, who loves taking part in quizzes and inventing wacky gadgets. Today he enjoys life to the full, and you would never guess that less than two years ago he was fighting a desperate battle with brain cancer.

Something wrong

The problems began when Amit started waking up with headaches. The headaches were especially bad in the morning, but by the evening he was usually feeling all right again. His doctor prescribed painkillers and told him to return if the problem continued.

Then, one weekend, Amit developed flulike symptoms and started running a fever and vomiting. There had been cases of the flu in the neighborhood, so his family was not too worried—until things got more serious. In the small hours of Sunday night Amit woke his parents to tell them he couldn't stand up straight and his vision was blurred. They rushed him straight to their local Accident and Emergency unit where a scan revealed the worrying truth. Amit had a tumor the size of a fist in his brain. "It was terrifying," his mother said. "We just couldn't believe it was happening."

More tests

Amit was transferred immediately to a specialist hospital where he was given a brain biopsy to find out whether the tumor was cancerous. This involved a small operation in which a tiny hole was made in his skull and a fine needle was used to remove a piece of the tumor to be tested in a lab. Amit's hearing, sight, and movement were also checked carefully to see how much the tumor had affected his body's nervous system. He was given an MRI scan to produce a detailed image of his brain.

Brain tumours

A brain tumor is an abnormal growth of cells within the brain, which can be either cancerous or benign. Each year about 40,000 in the United States are diagnosed with a cancerous brain tumor. Brain cancer is much more common among adults, but it does occur in children and teenagers. In the United States, approximately 2,000 children and adolescents are diagnosed with brain cancer each year. Cancerous tumors can be found in several different parts of the brain, but the most common types are found in the cerebellum, at the back of the skull, just above the neck.

Diagnosing the problem

Once the tests were completed, the doctors gave their official diagnosis. Amit had a cancerous

▲ Brain tumors can develop very rapidly. Some people with brain cancer experience no warning signs at all, until they suddenly become very ill. More frequently, people suffer from headaches and problems with their vision. These early symptoms alert them to the fact that there is something wrong with their brain.

tumor in the cerebellum—the area at the base of the brain that controls movement and balance. The tumor was causing pressure inside Amit's head, which was giving him headaches and causing his visual problems and vomiting. It was also starting to affect his sense of balance.

Brain surgery

Amit was given steroids—powerful drugs that had the effect of reducing the pressure inside his head. He was also prepared for an operation to remove his tumor. Before the surgeon operated, she explained that she would try to remove as much of the tumor as possible without damaging the surrounding brain tissue. Any cancerous cells that remained after surgery would be destroyed by chemotherapy and radiotherapy.

Amit's operation took almost four hours. When he came round from the anesthetic, his surgeon told him that she was very pleased with how the surgery had gone. She was confident that almost all the cancerous tissue had been removed, but she said they would still go ahead with the follow-up treatment—just to make sure that there were no stray cancer cells left in his brain.

Following up

As soon as he was strong enough after his operation, Amit started on a six-week course of chemotherapy. This was followed by daily sessions of radiotherapy, lasting for two weeks. Before the radiotherapy began, Amit was fitted with a special helmet so that the radioactive rays could be directed only at the area that had been affected by cancer.

By the end of his treatment, Amit was very weak and tired, but he was delighted to learn that he was completely free of cancer. Since then, all his check-ups, scans, and X-rays have shown that he has stayed in the clear.

Life after cancer

Amit has now taken up his old life again. Even though he missed a year of schooling, he had kept up with his classwork and homework, thanks to some excellent teachers on the ward. Nowadays you'd never guess that he had suffered from brain cancer, except for his new fascination with medical research.

▶ **This patient is being given a specialized form of radiotherapy, used for treating brain tumors. The patient's head is held in place by a metal frame, which keeps it completely still. The frame is adjusted so that the radiation targets the tumor, but does not affect other parts of the brain.**

Learning in hospital

Just because young people are in the hospital, it doesn't mean their schoolwork has to stop. Specially trained teachers help patients with their lessons and assign them projects and homework. Students benefit from one-to-one attention but also often study in groups.

Amit is also enjoying his old hobby of inventing gadgets. His latest invention is a mechanical grabber, operated by a simple handle, which can pick up things from the floor. It is designed to help people who have restricted movement in their hands as a result of brain cancer.

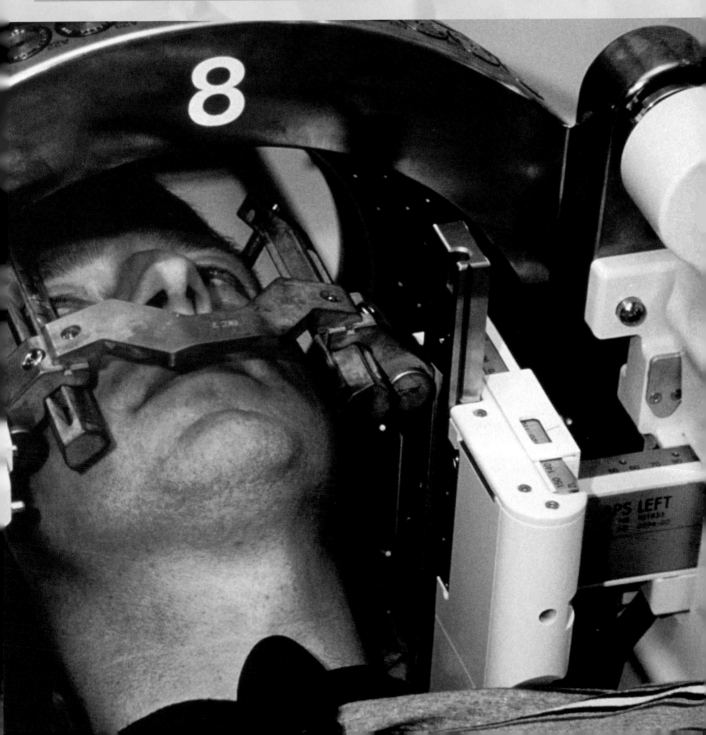

Sam's Story
Baseball Saw Me Through

Ever since he was six years old, Sam has loved baseball. He never missed a match and he would spend hours practising his swing. So when he started saying he was "too tired for baseball," his parents knew there was something wrong.

Feeling tired

In the months leading up to his tenth birthday, Sam began to experience sudden dizzy spells and his body ached all over. Then one day he collapsed. His parents rushed him to the hospital, where they were shocked to learn that he was suffering from advanced leukemia.

Going downhill

In just a few days, Sam's life changed completely. He was admitted to the cancer ward of his local hospital and put on an intensive course of chemotherapy. His family hoped that they would soon see an improvement, but instead Sam's condition grew rapidly worse. He developed a serious infection in his arm at the place where the drip was inserted and lost nearly 30 pounds (14 grams) in weight. When his friends visited him in hospital, they hardly recognized him—except that he was still wearing his beloved baseball cap.

A turning point

The lowest point came when Sam's parents were asked to come in for a meeting with his doctors. "We need to step up the treatment if we're going to beat the cancer," the doctors said. "And the only way to do that is to insert a Hickman line [see panel] in Sam's chest, so the drugs are delivered directly into his body."

The following day the doctors performed a small operation to insert the line, ready to begin a new stage of intensive treatment. When Sam came round from the anesthetic, his dad was by his bed with a special present. It was a catcher's chest protector that had

Hickman line

Patients who need to be given large doses of chemotherapy sometimes have a Hickman line inserted into their chest, so that the drugs can be delivered directly into their body. A Hickman line consists of a narrow tube that connects to one of the main veins leading to the heart. Once it is in place, a Hickman line can stay in the body for weeks or even months.

▶ For many young people, baseball is a way of life. Sam's passion for the sport helped him to get through a very difficult time in his life. Later, the team he supported became involved in fund-raising for young cancer patients.

been specially adapted to protect the Hickman line in Sam's chest—and it had been signed by all the players in his favorite team.

Sam wore the chest protector—and the Hickman line—for the next month, until it was obvious that he was going to pull through. Looking back on his experience four years later, he remembers: "I think it was that chest protector that saw me through. I felt as though all my heroes were rooting for me."

Josh's Story
Spreading the Word

For Josh, the discovery that he had brain cancer came very suddenly. One morning, as the family were sitting down to breakfast, he had a major epileptic seizure (see panel right). He had been feeling fine until then. Only the day before he had been playing soccer with his friends.

Emergency action

An ambulance was called and Josh was rushed to hospital where tests revealed a malignant tumor in his brain. Within a couple of days he was being prepared for major surgery. "It was all so quick," his dad remembers. 'One day we were enjoying a normal family life with three lively kids. The next day we had become a cancer family, spending all the time we could in the hospital with Josh.'

Epileptic seizures

An epileptic seizure is a sign that there is too much activity in the brain. It can have a range of causes, including pressure from a tumor. When someone has a seizure, they become unconscious, their muscles contract (go stiff and tight), and the person usually falls to the ground. Seizures usually only last for a few minutes. People who have repeated seizures are described as suffering from epilepsy.

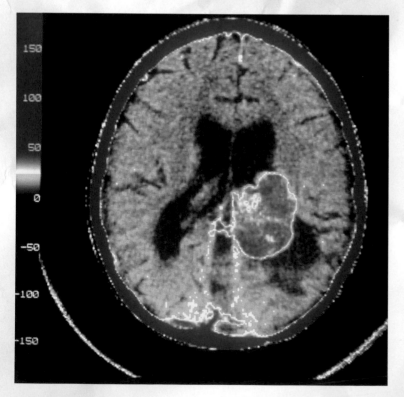

Josh's operation lasted for 12 hours. His tumor was located in a part of the brain that controlled movement, so his surgeon had to be extremely careful that he did not remove too much brain tissue. After the operation, Josh had to have a shunt inserted inside his

◀ **This CT scan shows a cancerous brain tumor, viewed from the top of the skull. Before surgeons operate, they take a range of scans of the patient's brain and study them very carefully. This allows them to pinpoint the exact size and position of the tumor, so they can plan their operation precisely.**

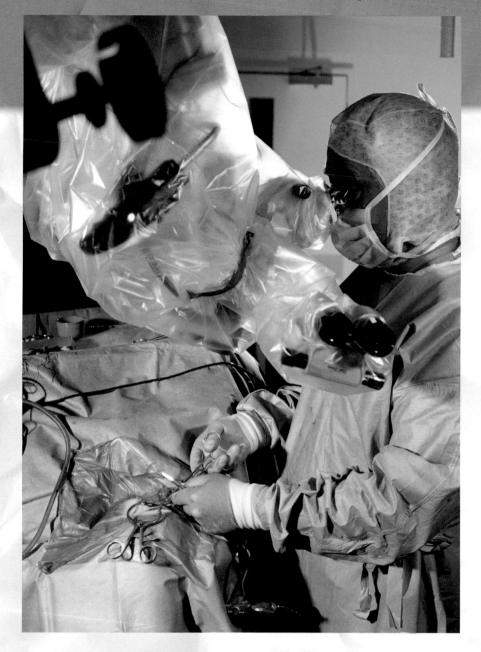

► A brain surgeon at work in a completely sterile (germ-free) environment. He is using a microscope to help him identify exactly what tissues should be removed from the patient's brain. This kind of very detailed operation is known as "microsurgery."

head. A shunt is a thin tube of rubber or plastic that is used to drain off excess fluid that collects inside the body.

A slow recovery

Two weeks later, Josh had another operation to remove the shunt, and then he started on the long, slow road to recovery. Following the operation it was clear that Josh's ability to think was just as good as before, but he had lost some movement in his left arm. He was given intensive physiotherapy, which brought back most of the movement, but he was left with a slight tremor (shaking) in his left hand.

Health problems

Josh also faced six months of chemotherapy and radiotherapy, which stretched into nine months because of other setbacks. As a result of the chemotherapy, his resistance to infection dropped so low that he caught pneumonia twice. Each time he had to stop the treatment until he was strong enough to continue. All these problems were discouraging, but Josh was determined that he would recover, and he gradually started gaining strength.

Home again

By the time he was ready to go home for good, Josh had been in the hospital for almost a year. The hospital was a long way from his home, and although his family made regular visits, he had lost touch with most of his friends at school. Josh was very keen to get back into his old life, but he dreaded having to explain to his classmates all the things that had happened to him. He also felt very self-conscious. His hair had not yet grown back after his chemotherapy and his left hand was shaky. All Josh wanted to do was to settle back into normal life, but he worried that he would appear very different to everyone else.

Back to school

Fortunately the return to school was not as hard as Josh had feared. The hospital had a special "back to school" scheme to support Josh and his family and to prepare the school for his return. A specially trained member of the hospital's staff went into the school to explain exactly what had happened to Josh while he had been away. She ended with a question-and-answer session, "so you won't have to bother Josh with endless questions."

When Josh went back to school, he was surprised how easy it was to fit in. All his friends saw him as a hero: "None of us have been through half as much as him." And within a few months, he was back in the soccer team.

Spreading the word

These days, Josh no longer feels shy when he talks about his cancer. In fact, he has started a cancer awareness campaign, visiting schools and youth groups to talk about his experience.

"I think it's important that people should understand more about cancer and its treatment," he says. "It's very helpful for kids who've just been diagnosed to know that there are plenty of others who understand exactly how they feel. I can show them that I have been there too. I've had cancer—and come out the other side."

"Back to school" schemes

Many cancer hospitals run a "back to school" scheme to make it easier for young people to return to school after their treatment. Trained members of staff hold sessions for classmates and teachers, informing them of any special requirements that the returning pupil might have. Depending on the age of the pupils, staff use a range of teaching tools, including puppet shows, videos, and written materials. The staff also give support to young people and their families while they are getting used to returning to school.

◄ Some young people decide to share their experience of cancer with others. By telling their own story they can raise awareness of the problems cancer patients face. They can also give hope to others who may develop cancer in the future.

Maya and Her Donor
A Special Friendship

Maya first developed leukemia when she was seven years old, and after a year's treatment she went into remission. For the next six years she was cancer-free. But then, when she was 13, the cancer returned—and this time her doctors decided to take a different approach.

"You need a transplant"

When Maya went into the hospital for the second time, her doctors explained that they needed to tackle the source of the problem. The marrow inside her bones was working overtime to produce the cancer cells that passed into her blood. In order to beat the cancer, she needed a total bone marrow transplant.

Maya was given intensive chemotherapy to kill off all the diseased cells in her own bone marrow. At the same time the records of bone marrow donors were searched to find the perfect match for her. Fortunately they found an ideal donor— a young woman who lived in a city hundreds of miles away.

Marrow donor

Five years earlier, a college student named Rose had heard a radio show asking for bone marrow donors and had decided to sign up.

"I figured that I had been incredibly lucky in my life and I wanted to give someone else the chance to have a good future."

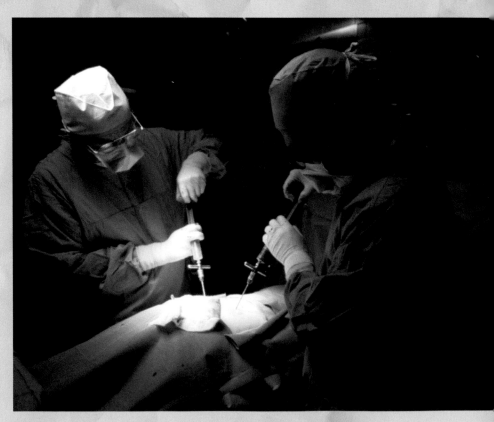

▲ These doctors are "harvesting" healthy bone marrow from a donor, ready to be transplanted into the bones of a cancer patient. Marrow is sucked out of the hip bones using large syringes.

Bone marrow transplants

A bone marrow transplant involves a minor operation on the donor, in which a syringe is inserted into the bone and liquid marrow is removed. Altogether about a litre of bone marrow is removed and frozen. The frozen marrow is then transported in a sterile (germ-free) container to the hospital where it is needed. Then it is injected into the bone marrow of the person with cancer. Once it has entered into the patient's bones, the healthy bone marrow can start to produce normal blood cells.

When she got the call to come into hospital and donate her bone marrow, Rose didn't hesitate—and within a few days Maya had received Rose's gift of life. Along with the bone marrow came a letter from Rose sending her best wishes. The transplant was successful, and—thanks to Rose—Maya made a very good recovery.

Following the rules on marrow donation, Rose did not reveal her identity, and when Maya wrote back reporting on her progress, she also kept her real name secret. But after a year the rules allowed them to reveal their identities—so long as they both agreed. By that time they had developed a firm friendship and were keen to meet. "I couldn't wait to see the friend who had given me back my life," said Maya.

A special meeting

Fourteen months after Rose had given her bone marrow, she traveled to the city where Maya lived. It was an emotional meeting for both of them. As Maya put it, "Even though I had never set eyes on Rose before, I felt I knew her really well. After all—I have a part of her inside me!"

▶ Bone marrow donors and recipients have a very special bond. Not all patients choose to be in touch with their donors, but some donors and recipients develop a close friendship.

Tom and Megan's Story
Cancer in the Family

Tom was 14 when his younger sister Megan (then age six) was diagnosed with a brain tumor. It was the start of a long and difficult period for the family. His dad remembers that time very clearly, "When Megan got sick, it was very hard for Tom, but he was amazing. He really helped her to pull through."

Facing it together

Right from the start of Megan's treatment, Tom insisted that he wanted to be involved. He visited her in hospital as often as he could and told her jokes and stories to keep her cheerful. He even created a special cartoon for her, starring Mighty Megan fighting the Big Bad Cancer Monster.

Families under stress

When a child has cancer, everyone in the family is affected. It is not unusual for the brothers and sisters of the cancer patient to feel neglected as their parents are forced to concentrate all their time and energy on the child who is ill. In some cases, families even have to be split up, with children going to stay with relatives so their parents can spend more time in hospital. There are a number of support groups that provide help and practical support for families coping with cancer. Turn to page 45 to find websites with links to support groups.

When Megan came home from hospital for visits, Tom spent hours with her playing games and watching her favorite TV shows. He encouraged her to take her medicines by mixing up tempting ice cream flavors to help disguise the taste, and when Megan's long, curly hair started falling out, he made a pact with her. They would both have their heads shaved together so there would be two "baldies" in the family.

Raising money

Tom also decided to take part in a fundraising race organized by the hospital where Megan was treated. He had a T-shirt made with his sister's face and the words "Running for Megan" printed on it, and he managed to persuade dozens of people to sponsor him—including many local stores and businesses.

On the day of the race, Tom was the top fundraiser. Even though she was very weak, Megan insisted on being there to see him cross the finishing line. Later that day she made a promise to Tom that one day she would run the race with him.

Continued support

Megan's recovery wasn't easy. After 18 months of treatment, her doctors reported that she was in remission, and family life began to return to normal, but two years later the cancer came back and she had to go back to the hospital. Through all the ups and downs, Tom continued to support his sister, although there were times when he wished that his parents could spend more time with him.

Eventually, Megan was declared completely free of cancer, and since then she has stayed very healthy. Tom is now grown up and no longer lives at home, but he still returns every summer for a special event. Each July he takes part in the annual fundraising run for Megan's hospital. And, for the last three years, Megan and Tom have run the race together.

◄ **Families can make an enormous difference to the way a young cancer patient feels. If you're feeling scared and isolated, it's great to have the support of everyone at home— and to have a brother or sister to talk to.**

Amy's Story
Losing Dad

Amy's dad had always had a nasty "smoker's cough," but when the coughing suddenly became much worse he was sent to the hospital for tests. The results came through a few days before Amy's 13th birthday. Her dad had tumors in both his lungs, and the cancer had spread to his stomach. His doctors said he only had a few months to live.

A difficult time

The next few weeks passed in a daze for Amy. Whenever she could, she went to the hospital to visit her dad. She was also kept very busy at home, helping to look after her two younger brothers. On top of all that Amy still went to school. Her parents insisted that her life should continue as normally as possible.

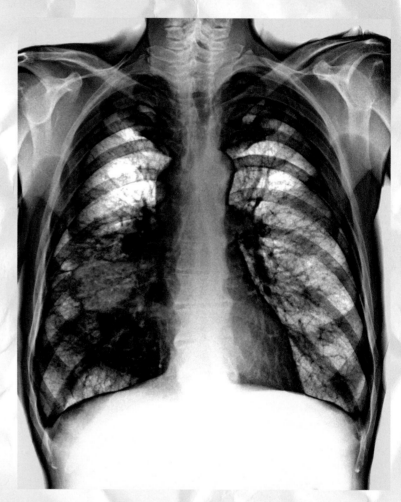

▶ This colored X-ray shows the chest of a patient with lung cancer. You can see a large tumor on the right lung, colored red. This kind of cancer is usually caused by smoking. Lung cancer almost never occurs in children or teenagers.

Lung cancer and smoking

Sufferers from lung cancer develop cancerous tumors inside their lungs. These tumors can grow rapidly, making breathing very difficult. Most cases of lung cancer cannot be cured, although chemotherapy and radiotherapy can slow the progress of the disease. Cigarette smoking is the cause of nearly all lung cancers. However, when people give up smoking, their risk of developing lung cancer drops dramatically. If they continue as nonsmokers, their risk of developing cancer will decrease steadily over the next ten years.

And in fact Amy felt relieved that school was just the same as it had always been. "My friends were very sympathetic, and I sometimes talked about Dad, but most of the time we talked about other things."

Last weeks

After a couple of months, it became clear that Amy's dad did not have much longer to live. The family decided that he should be at home for the last few weeks of his life. His bed was moved into the living room, and a specially trained nurse came to stay to give him all the care that he needed and make sure that he remained free from pain.

Good memories

Amy remembers her dad's last weeks as a very special time. "Of course we were sad, but we also had a lot of laughs. We got out all the photo albums and talked about all the good things we had done together. And Dad told us all our favorite jokes and stories."

Before her dad died he had several talks with Amy about her hopes for the future. He said he would always be proud of her and he told her to think of him giving her lots of love and strength. "I miss Dad every day, but I also feel that he is still part of me. We talk about him a lot and we all have our own memories of him."

► **After her dad died, Amy was very sad, but she had some great memories of him. She made up her mind that she would never smoke, and run the risk of developing lung cancer.**

Abi's Story
Cancer Nurse

Abi was nine years old when she was first diagnosed with lymphoma, and she spent her tenth birthday in the hospital. Everyone said she would be home in plenty of time for her next birthday, but she wasn't. Altogether she spent almost two years in the hospital before she was declared to be in remission. But her story didn't end there…

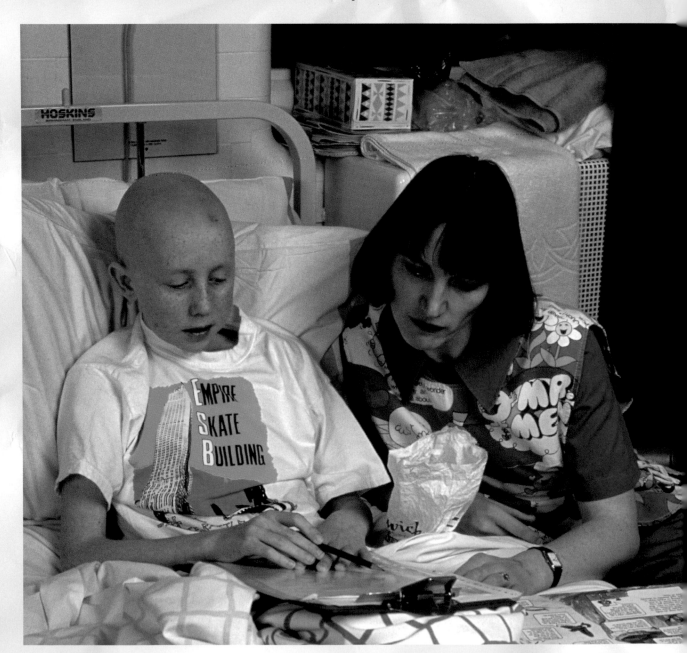

Hospital again

Over the next couple of years Abi returned to the hospital for frequent checkups, and the news was always good. But then, at the age of 13, she began to feel tired and ill again. Her tests showed that the cancer had metastasized (traveled) into her bone marrow and spleen.

Once again Abi was admitted to the hospital—this time on a teenage ward—and she began a lengthy course of treatment. Over the next 18 months she had an operation to remove her spleen, a bone marrow transplant, and intensive chemotherapy and radiotherapy. She made several very good friends on the ward and, alongside her treatment, she kept up with her schoolwork. "There were many good times, as well as bad," she said.

Home at last

Eventually, Abi was given a clean bill of health, and she returned to life at home. At first she found it hard to believe that she was cancer free, but as the years went by she felt more relaxed. "Having cancer makes you live each day to the full, because you never know what's around the corner, but I also began to look ahead to the future."

Choosing nursing

When the time came to choose a career, Abi had no problem in making up her mind. She decided she wanted to train as a nurse specializing in oncology (the treatment of cancer). Some people were surprised at Abi's choice, thinking she would want to put her hospital years behind her, but she was certain. "The nurses I met in hospital got so much out of their job, they wouldn't have changed it for anything. I know I've made the right decision."

Abi hopes that when she has finished her training she will be able to work on a ward with children and teenagers. "Because the patients usually stay for a long time, there's a chance to get to know them really well."

◀ Nurses who work on cancer wards become well acquainted with their patients. Not only do they look after their patients' physical needs, they also have time to talk and play games with them. Many young patients become great friends with their nurses and come back to see them even after they have finished their treatment.

Cancer nursing

Nurses who specialize in oncology undertake several years of training. During their training they learn all about the many types of cancer and the range of treatments available. They also take courses in managing pain and in giving psychological support. Some nurses specialize in a particular aspect of cancer care, such as chemotherapy. Pediatric cancer nurses help children with cancer, and their families, providing support at home and in the hospital.

Glossary

abnormal Not normal and not healthy.

anesthetic A drug that makes you unconscious or pain-free during an operation.

antibiotics Drugs that are used to fight infections.

benign Harmless and not dangerous.

biopsy A small operation to remove some cells from a patient's body, so they can be tested and examined under a microscope.

bone graft A piece of bone that is taken from another part of a patient's body and used to replace diseased or damaged bone.

bone marrow The jellylike substance inside your bones that creates new blood cells.

cancerous Affected by cancer.

cell A tiny part of an animal or plant, which can only be seen under a microscope. All living things are made up of cells.

chemotherapy A treatment for cancer that uses a combination of medical drugs to destroy the cancerous cells.

CT scan A scan that uses X-ray beams, sent from different angles, to build up a 3-D photograph of the inside of the body. CT stands for computerized tomography.

diagnose Identify a disease or disorder in a patient.

donor Somebody who gives something to others in order to help them.

infection An illness caused by germs.

intensive Involving concentrated effort to achieve something.

leukemia A type of cancer that affects the blood. When people have leukemia, their bone marrow produces abnormal blood cells that multiply very fast and crowd out the healthy cells.

lymphoma A type of cancer that attacks the body's lymph system and stops it from fighting infection.

MRI scan A scan that uses magnetism to build up a picture of the different tissues inside the body. MRI stands for magnetic resonance imaging.

nervous system The system of nerves that connects the brain to all the other parts of the body.

oncology The study and treatment of cancer. Specialists who treat patients with cancer are called oncologists.

organ A part of the body that does a particular job, such as the heart, liver, or lungs.

osteosarcoma A type of cancer that attacks the bones.

partial remission A state of being partly (but not completely) recovered from a disease.

physiotherapy Special exercises designed to make the body stronger.

pneumonia A serious lung disease that makes breathing very difficult.

prosthesis An artificial element that replaces a leg or an arm or a part of a limb. A prosthesis (or prosthetic device) can be a rod inserted into a limb, or it can be an artifical limb, hand, or foot.

psychological Connected with the mind and the way that people think and behave.

radioactive Sending out powerful rays that can be used to destroy cancer cells.

radiotherapy A treatment for cancer in which high-energy X-rays are directed at parts of the body in order to destroy cancer cells.

reject React violently against something. Patients often have to take special drugs to stop their body from rejecting a transplant.

remission Recovery from a disease. When people are 'in remission' from cancer, their bodies are no longer producing cancerous cells.

shin The large leg bone that connects the kneecap to the ankle.

spleen A small organ on the left-hand side of the body that helps to fight infection.

surgery The act of cutting someone open in order to remove, repair, or replace body parts.

syringe A tube with a plunger and a hollow needle, used for giving injections and for drawing out blood or bone marrow.

tissue The flesh and muscle that make up a human body.

transplant A bone marrow transplant is an operation to replace a patient's diseased bone marrow with healthy bone marrow given by a donor. Doctors can also transplant organs such as a heart, a liver, or a kidney.

tumor A swelling or lump caused by the abnormal growth of a group of cells. Some tumors are cancerous. Others are harmless.

visualize Form a visual image of something in the mind.

X-rays Beams of energy that can pass through solid things. X-rays are often used to produce a photograph of the inside of a person's body.

Further Information

Books
Biology of Cancer: Diagnosis and Treatment of Cancer by Lyman Lyons (Chelsea House, 2007)

Deadly Diseases and Epidemics: Cervical Cancer by Juliet Spender (Chelsea House, 2006)

Fighting For My Life: Growing Up With Cancer by Amy M. Mareck (Fairview Press, 2007)

Health Issues: Cancer by Kirsten Lamb (Wayland, 2007)

Teen's Guides: Living with Cancer by ZoAnn Dreyer (Facts on File, 2008)

Websites
www.cancer.org

The website of the American Cancer Society. The site provides information about cancer and links to local groups.

www.cancerresearchuk.org

The website of Cancer Research UK. The site gives information for cancer patients, and has news of the latest medical research.

www.planetcancer.org

Teens with cancer, but who have "a lot of living to do," share stories, advice, and jokes with each other.

www.jimmyteens.tv

A place for young people to share their experiences of cancer through videos and blogs.

www.livestrong.org

The Lance Armstrong Foundation, set up by the champion bike racer (and cancer survivor) unites people "to fight cancer believing that unity is strength, knowledge is power, and attitude is everything."

www.teensagainstcancer.org

Teenagers from the South Bay area of California keep the public aware of issues relating to childhood cancer, with lots of information and advice about fundraising.

Index